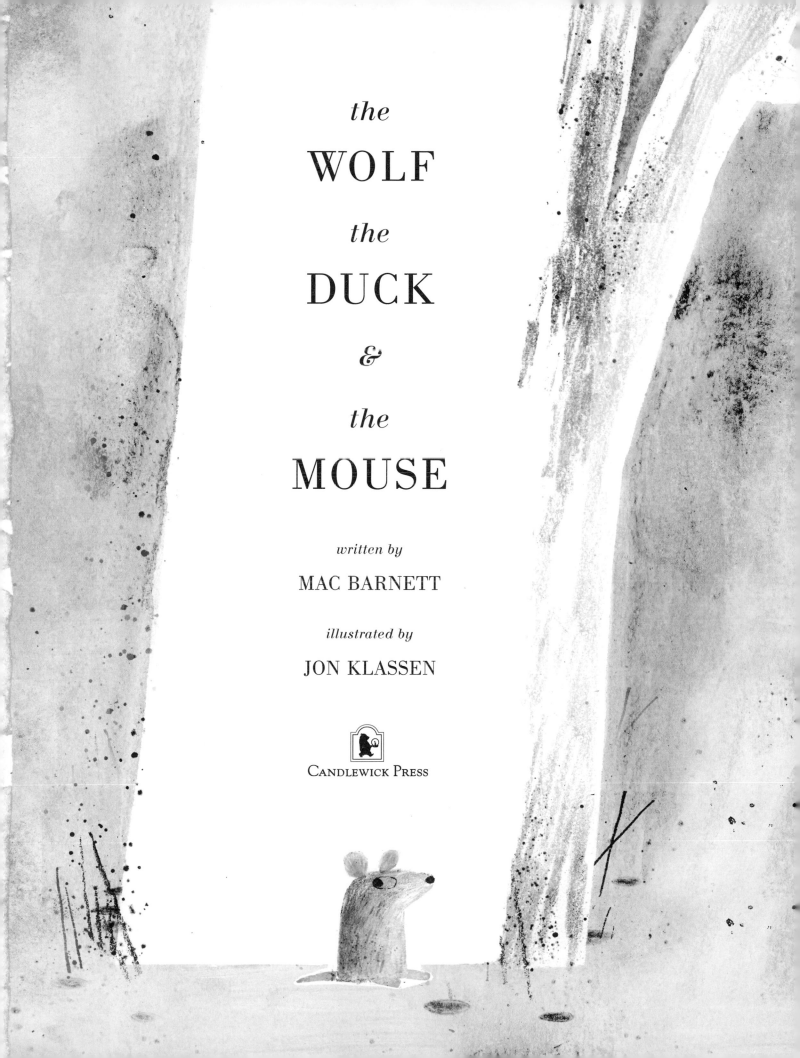

the WOLF

the DUCK

&

the MOUSE

written by

MAC BARNETT

illustrated by

JON KLASSEN

CANDLEWICK PRESS

Early one morning, a mouse

met a wolf,

and he was quickly gobbled up.

"Oh woe!" said the mouse.

"Oh me! Here I am, caught

in the belly of the beast.

I fear this is the end."

"Be quiet!" someone shouted.

"I'm trying to sleep."

The mouse shrieked, "Who's there?"

A light was lit. A duck lay in bed.

"Well?" said the duck.

"Oh," said the mouse.

"Is that all?" asked the duck.

"It's the middle of the night."

The mouse looked around.

"Well, out there it's morning."

"It is?" said the duck. "It's so hard to tell.

I do wish this belly had a window or two.

In any case, breakfast!"

The meal was delicious.

"Where did you get jam?" the mouse asked.

"And a tablecloth?"

The duck munched a crust.

"You'd be surprised what you find inside
 of a wolf."

"It's nice," said the mouse.

"It's home," said the duck.

"You live here?"

"I live well! I may have been swallowed,
 but I have no intention of being eaten."

For lunch they made soup.

The mouse cleared his throat.

"Do you miss the outside?"

"I do not!" said the duck.

"When I was outside, I was afraid every day
wolves would swallow me up.

In here, that's no worry."

The duck had a point.

"Can I stay?" the mouse asked.

"Of course!" the duck said.

This called for a dance.

The ruckus inside made the wolf's stomach ache.
"Oh woe!" said the wolf. "Oh shame! Never
have I felt such aching and pain. Surely it must
have been something I ate."

The duck shouted up, "I have a cure!"

"You do?" asked the wolf.

"Yes! An old remedy sure to settle your tummy. Eat a hunk of good cheese. And a flagon of wine! And some beeswax candles."

That night they feasted.

The duck made a toast. "To the health of the wolf!"

But the wolf felt worse.

"I feel like I'll burst. It hurts just to move."

A hunter heard the wolf moan.

He fired a shot but missed in the dark.

The duck called up, "Run! Run for our lives!"

The wolf tried to escape,
but he tripped
and got trapped in an
old oak tree's roots.

"Oh woe!" said the duck. "Oh doom!

What can we do? I fear this is the end."

The mouse stood up.

"We must fight. We must try.

Tonight we ride to defend our home."

"CHARGE!"

"Oh woe!" said the hunter. "Oh death!
These woods are full of evil and wraiths!"
He fled from the forest and never returned.

The wolf bowed down
to the duck and the mouse.
"You saved my life
when I thought not
to spare yours.
Ask a favor of me.
I will be glad to grant it."

Well,

you can guess what they asked for.

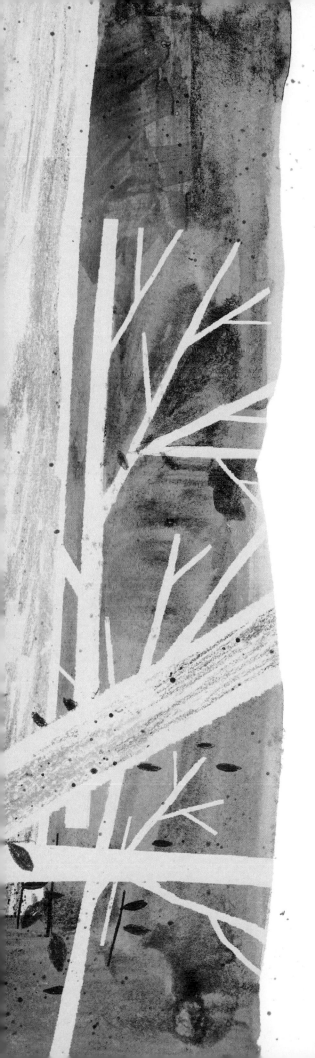

And that's why the wolf howls at the moon.

"Oh woe! Oh woe!"

Every night he howls at the moon.

"Oh woe!"

For Christian Robinson—M. B.

For Mac—J. K.

First edition 2017

Library of Congress Catalog Card Number pending
ISBN 978-0-7636-7754-1

17 18 19 20 21 22 APS 10 9 8 7 6 5 4 3 2 1

Printed in Humen, Dongguan, China

FSC
www.fsc.org
MIX
Paper from
responsible sources
FSC® C101537

This book was typeset in Bodoni.
The illustrations were done in mixed media.

Candlewick Press
99 Dover Street
Somerville, Massachusetts 02144

visit us at www.candlewick.com